Robert Munsch

Illustrated by Michael Martchenko

Up, Up, Down

Cartwheel
·B·O·O·K·S·®

SCHOLASTIC INC.

New York   Toronto   London   Auckland   Sydney
Mexico City   New Delhi   Hong Kong

The illustrations in this book were painted in watercolor on Arches paper.
This book was designed in QuarkXPress,
with type set in 20 point Caslon 224 Medium.

Text copyright © 2001 by Bob Munsch Enterprises, Ltd.
Illustrations copyright © 2001 by Michael Martchenko.
All rights reserved. Published by Scholastic Inc.
Published simultaneously in Canada by Scholastic Canada Ltd.

SCHOLASTIC, CARTWHEEL BOOKS,
and associated logos are trademarks and/or registered trademarks of Scholastic Inc.
Band-Aid is a trademark of Johnson & Johnson.

Library of Congress Cataloging-in-Publication Data
Munsch, Robert N., 1945-
    Up, up, down by Robert Munsch ; illustrated by Michael Martchenko.
        p. cm.
    "Cartwheel books."
    Summary: Despite the warnings of her mother and father, Anna persists in trying to
climb things, until she gets to the top of a tall tree.
    ISBN 0-439-18770-2 (hc)
    [1. Tree climbing--Fiction.] I. Martchenko, Michael, ill. II. Title

PZ7.M927 Up 2001
[E]--dc21   00-04052

        12 11 10 9 8 7 6 5 4 3 2 1   01 02 03 04 05
                        Printed in Canada
                        First printing, April 2001

To Anna James, Guelph, Ontario
— R.M.

One day Anna, who liked to climb, walked into the kitchen and started to climb up the refrigerator.

She went

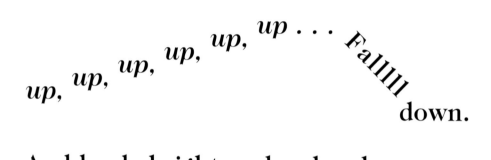

up, *up,* *up,* *up,* *up,* *up* . . . Fallll down.

And landed right on her head.

"OW OUCH! OW OUCH! OW OUCH!"

Anna's mother saw her and said,
"Be careful! Don't climb!"

But Anna didn't listen. She went to her bedroom and tried to climb up her dresser.

She went

up, up, up, up, up, up . . . Fallllll down.

And landed right on her tummy.

"OW OUCH! OW OUCH! OW OUCH!"

Her father found her on the floor and said, "Be careful! Don't climb."

So Anna decided to go outside where it was okay to climb, and the biggest thing she could find to climb was . . .

The Tree.

Anna went

up, up, up, up, up, up . . . Fallllll down.

And landed right on her bottom.

"OW OUCH! OW OUCH! OW OUCH!"

But the next time she was very careful.
She went

up, *up,* *up,* *up,* *up,* *up,* *up* . . .

all the way to the top of the tree.

And then Anna yelled,
"I'm the king of the castle,
Mommy's a dirty rascal!"

Anna's mother came out of the house
and looked all around. She said,
"Anna? Anna? Anna?

ANNA!
Get out of that tree!"

And Anna said, "No, no, no, no, no!"

So her mother tried to climb the tree.
She went

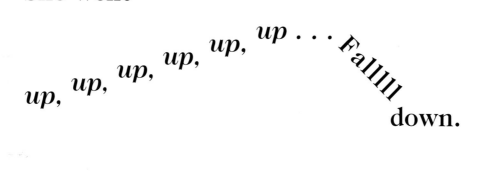

up, up, up, up, up, up . . . Fallll down.

And landed right on her head.

"OW OUCH! OW OUCH! OW OUCH!"

And then Anna yelled, "I'm the king of the castle, Daddy's a dirty rascal!"

Anna's father came out of the house and looked all around.

He said, "Anna? Anna? Anna?

ANNA!
Get out of that tree!"

And Anna said, "No, no, no, no, no!"

So her father tried to climb the tree.
He went

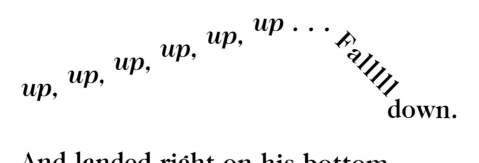

down.

And landed right on his bottom.

Anna leaned over the side of the tree. She looked at her mother and she looked at her father. Her mother was holding her head and yelling,

"WAHHHHH!"

And her father was holding his bottom and yelling,

"OW OW OW OW OW!"

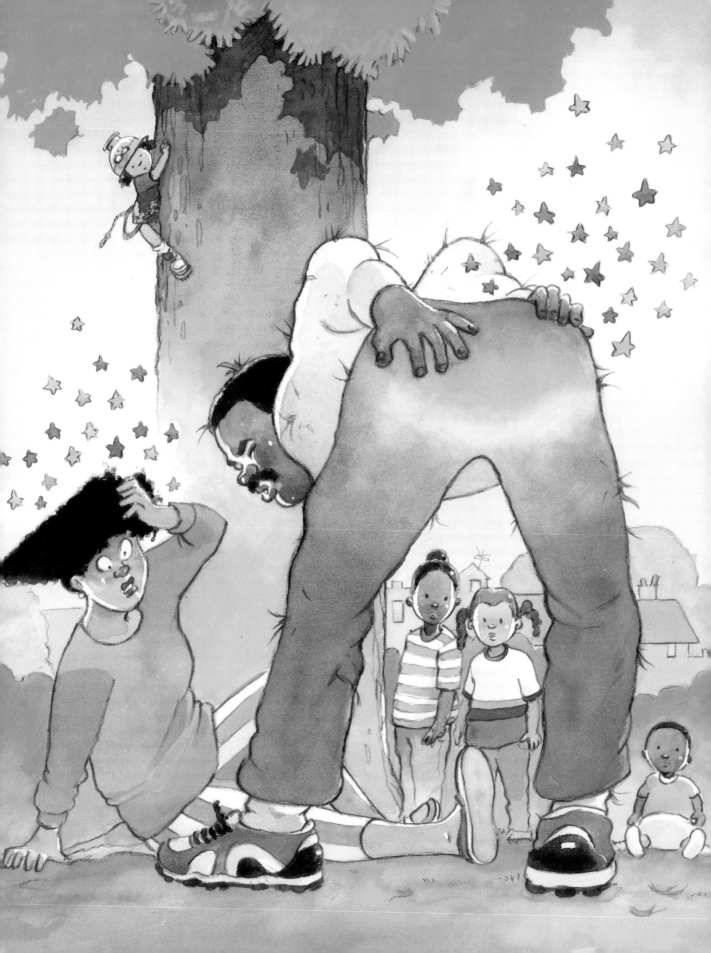

Then Anna climbed

down, down, down, down, down, down,

all the way to the bottom of the tree.
She got her brother and sisters, and
they ran inside and got ten enormous
Band-Aids.

26

Anna walked over to her mother, took the paper off one Band-Aid:

SCRITCH!

And wrapped it around her mother's head:

WRAP WRAP WRAP WRAP WRAP.

Then Anna walked over to her father, took the paper off the other Band-Aid:

SCRITCH!

And wrapped it around her father's bottom:

WRAP WRAP WRAP WRAP WRAP.

Then Anna looked at her mother and
she looked at her father and she said,

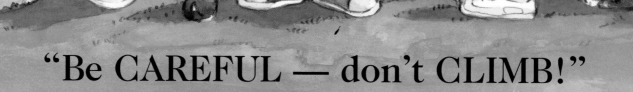

"Be CAREFUL — don't CLIMB!"